DiNo School

Say Cheese, Teddy Rex!

by Bonnie Williams • illustrated by John Gordon

Ready-to-Read

Simon Spotlight
New York London Toronto Sydney New Delhi

SIMON SPOTLIGHT
An imprint of Simon & Schuster Children's Publishing Division
1230 Avenue of the Americas, New York, New York 10020
This Simon Spotlight edition July 2016
Copyright © 2016 Simon & Schuster, Inc.
SIMON SPOTLIGHT, READY-TO-READ, and colophon are registered trademarks of Simon & Schuster, Inc.
For information about special discounts for bulk purchases, please contact Simon & Schuster
Special Sales at 1-866-506-1949 or business@simonandschuster.com.
Manufactured in the United States of America 0616 LAK
10 9 8 7 6 5 4 3 2 1
This book has been cataloged with the Library of Congress.
ISBN 978-1-4814-6609-7 (pbk)
ISBN 978-1-4814-6610-3 (hc)
ISBN 978-1-4814-6611-0 (eBook)

Today is a big day!
Today is picture day
at Dino School.

The dinosaurs are dressed
in their best outfits.

Val the Velociraptor wears
her prettiest bow.

Steve the Stegosaurus
makes sure his spikes
stand up straight.

Teddy the Tyrannosaurus rex
has on his favorite shirt.
There are stars on it.

Pete the Pterodactyl helps
Teddy count the stars.
"1, 2, 3, 4, 5," counts Pete.

"Time to line up,"
says Ms. G.
The tallest dinosaurs
stand in the back row.

The smallest dinosaurs
stand in the front row.
Teddy smiles.
Everyone will see his stars!

Tina the Triceratops is late.

She is running.

She is holding
a cup of juice.

She trips.

Teddy looks down.

His shirt is ruined!

The stars are gone.

Teddy is mad.

Teddy is sad.

He starts to roar

and cry at the same time.

Tina wants to fix
her mistake.
What can she do?

Tina has an idea.

"We can cover the stain

with one big star."

Tina colors.

Val cuts.

Pete tapes.

Teddy has a brand-new star.

He cannot see the stain.

"I am sorry that I spilled,"

Tina tells Teddy.

"I am sorry
that I roared,"
Teddy tells Tina.
"Thank you for my
new star."

Tina and Teddy hug.
"I am very proud
of both of you,"
says Ms. G.
"Now, is everyone ready?"

"Yes!" says Teddy.

The dinosaurs line up
again.
Teddy stands right
in front.

His star shines
and so does his smile.

Say cheese, Teddy Rex!